P9-DCO-682

TRUCK

Donald Crews

Copyright © 1980 by Donald Crews.
All rights reserved. No part of this
book may be reproduced without permission
from the Publisher, Greenwillow Books,
10 East 53rd Street,
New York, NY 10022.
Manufactured in the USA.
13 14 15 16 LP 15 14 13

Greenwillow Books/New York

Library of Congress Cataloging in Publication Data
Crews, Donald. Truck. [1. Trucks–Pictorial works.
2. Stories without words] I. Title. PZ7. C8682Tr
[E] 79-19031 ISBN 978-0-688-80244-8
ISBN 978-0-688-84244-4 lib. bdg. ISBN 978-0-688-10481-8 pbk.

The art was prepared in four halftone separations
combined with black line drawings.

To A/N/A/D/J/M and especially Malcolm

T
O

RUCKING

TRUCKING

ONE WAY
STOP

EZ

TRUCKI

CKING

TOLCO
LIQUID GAS

12'6"
TUNNEL
AHEAD

CITYLINE

TRU
SPEED
LIMIT
40

TUNNEL
EXIT
ENTER
TRUCKING

NG
CL

PPER

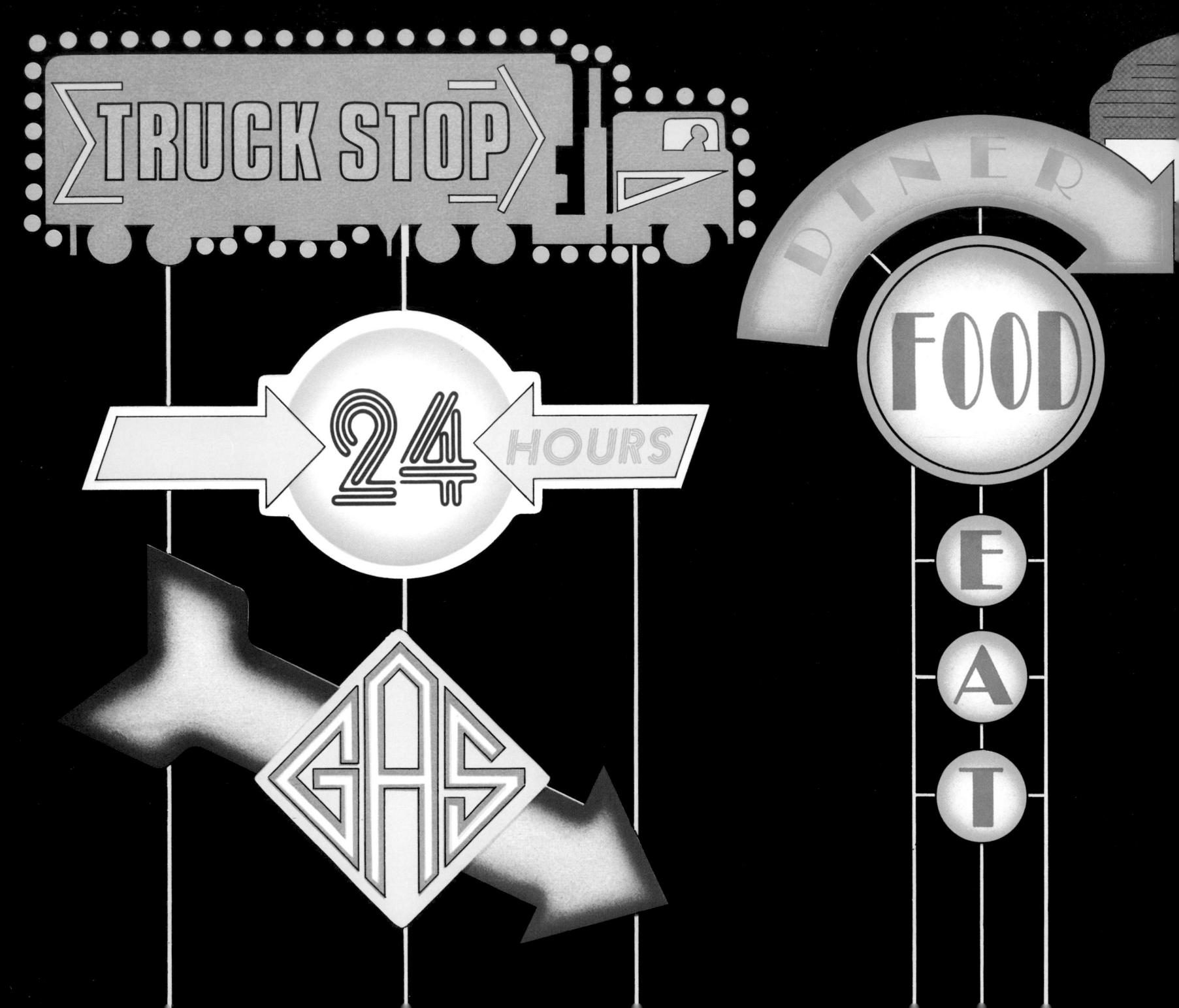
TRUCK STOP
DINER
FOOD
24 HOURS
EAT
GAS

DINER
TRUCKING
DIESEL
ONLY

TRUCKING

101
NORTH

TRUCKING
LIVESTOCK

Bakery
MOVING
79 T
G
HIGHWAY

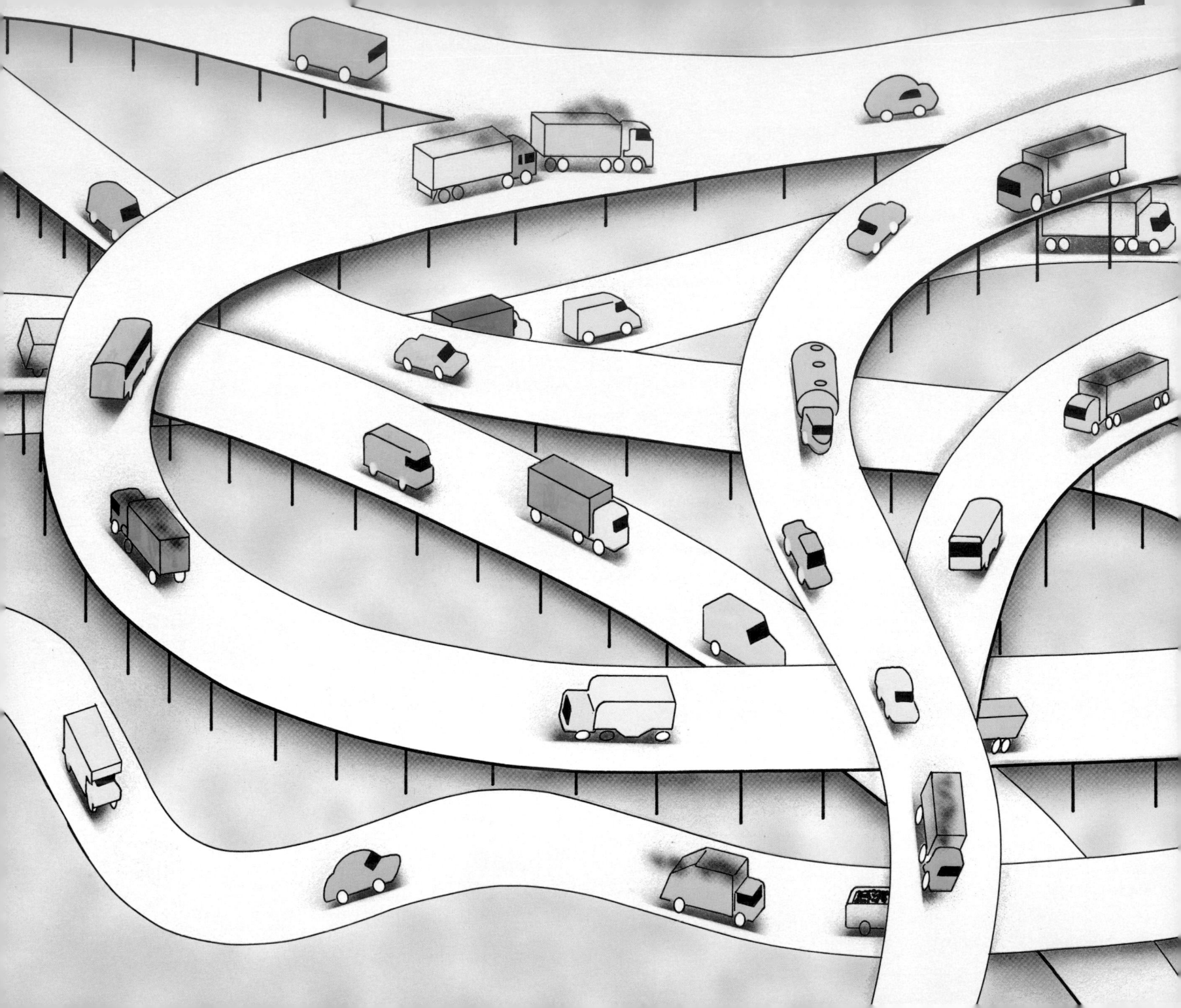

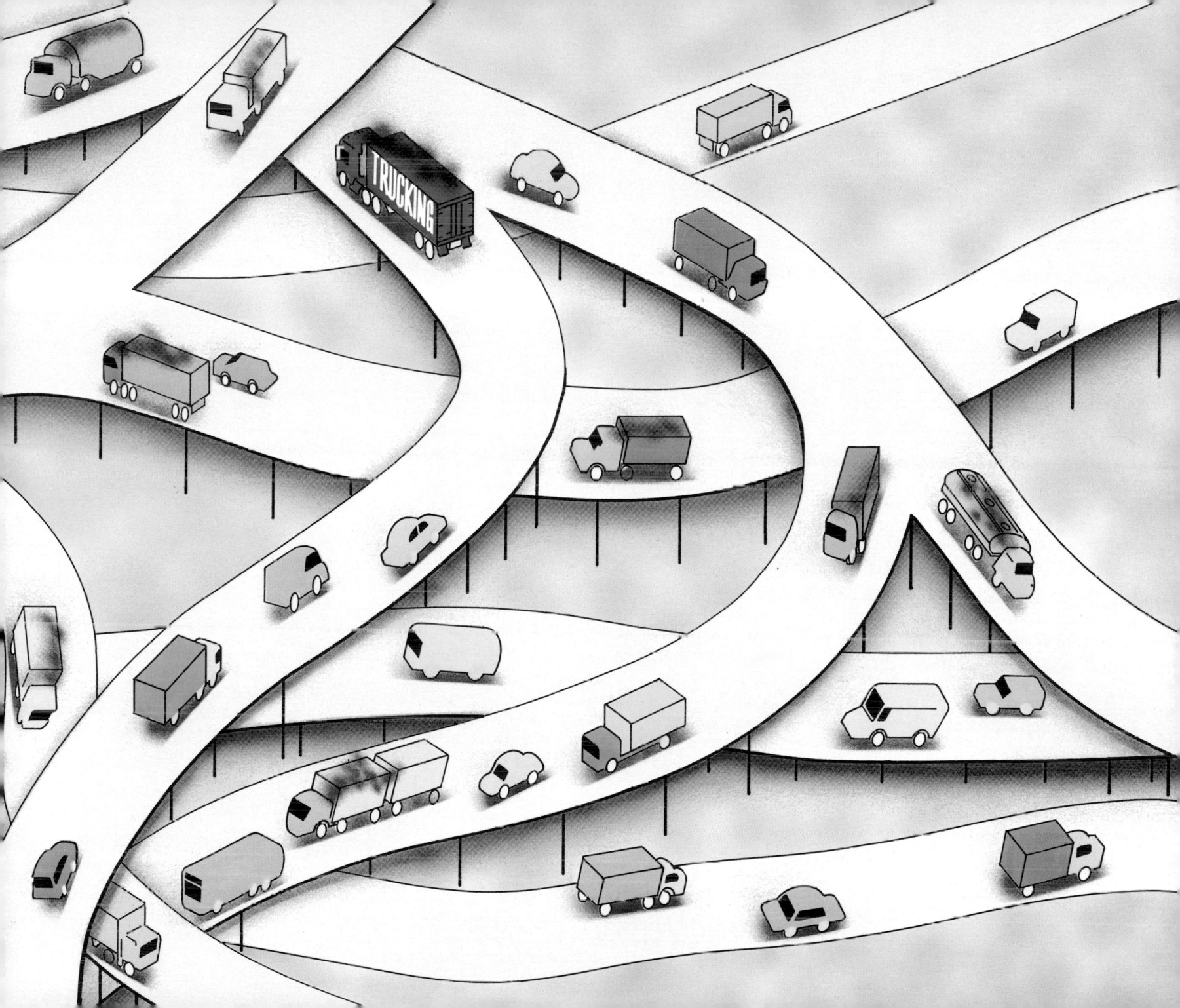
TRUCKING

TRUCKING

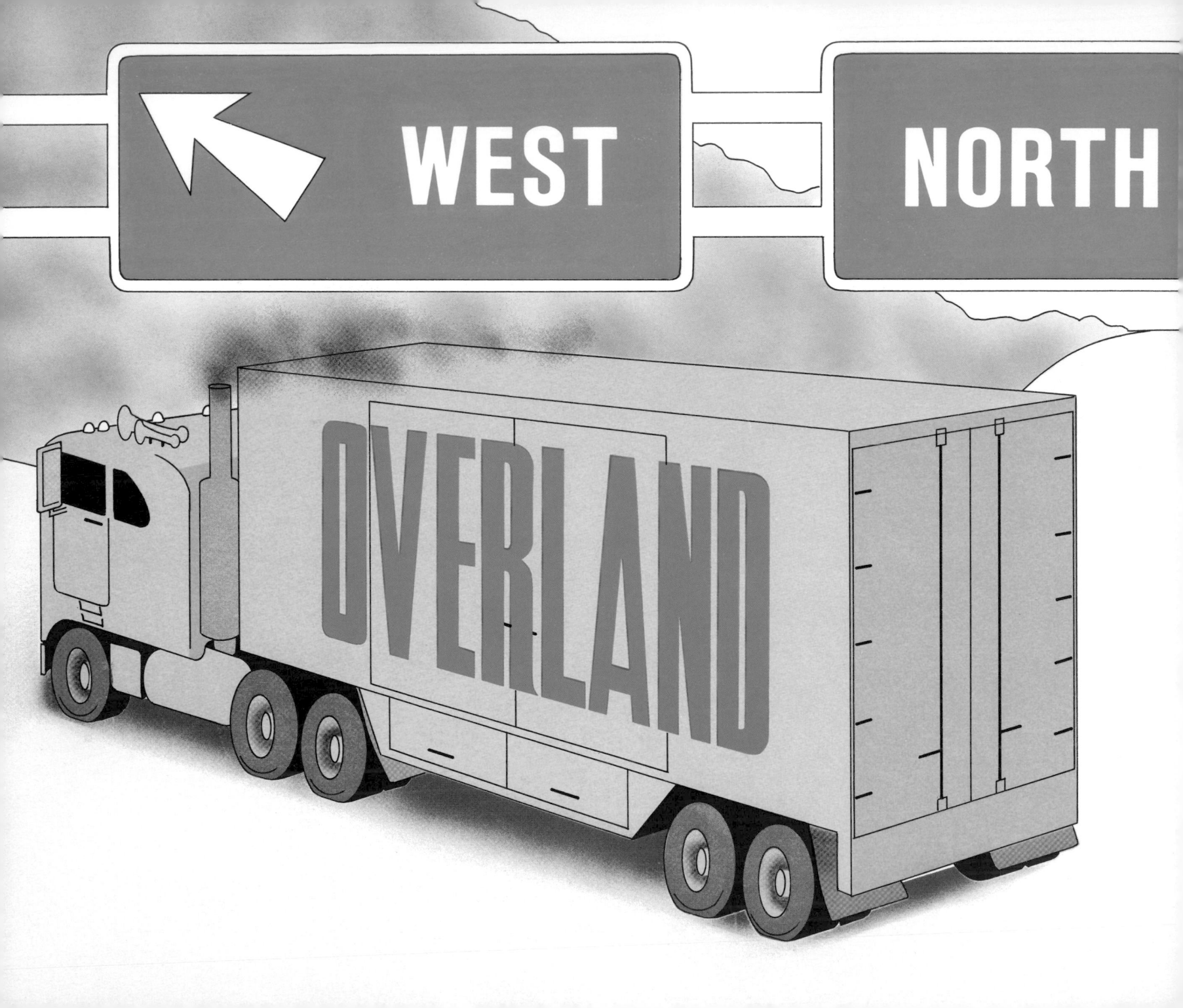
WEST
NORTH
OVERLAND

EAST
TRUCKING

TRUCKIN